Samuel H. Winter

Elementary Geometrical Drawing

Part I

SALZWASSER
VERLAG

Samuel H. Winter

Elementary Geometrical Drawing
Part I

Reprint of the original, first published in 1859.

1st Edition 2022 | ISBN: 978-3-37513-248-4

Verlag (Publisher): Salzwasser Verlag GmbH, Zeilweg 44, 60439 Frankfurt, Deutschland
Vertretungsberechtigt (Authorized to represent): E. Roepke, Zeilweg 44, 60439 Frankfurt, Deutschland
Druck (Print): Books on Demand GmbH, In de Tarpen 42, 22848 Norderstedt, Deutschland

ELEMENTARY

GEOMETRICAL DRAWING.

PART I.

ELEMENTARY

GEOMETRICAL DRAWING.

PART I.

INCLUDING PRACTICAL PLANE GEOMETRY, THE CONSTRUCTION OF SCALES,

THE USE OF THE SECTOR, THE MARQUOIS SCALES, AND

THE PROTRACTOR.

DESIGNED FOR THE

USE OF STUDENTS PREPARING FOR THE MILITARY EXAMINATIONS.

BY SAMUEL H. WINTER

MILITARY TUTOR.

LONDON

LONGMAN, GREEN, LONGMAN, AND ROBERTS

1859

ADVERTISEMENT.

THE following short outline of the First Part of Elementary Geometrical Drawing has been published with the view of supplying a want which the writer has long experienced in preparing Candidates for Military Examinations. It contains a portion of a MS. which has been used with advantage for a considerable period amongst his own pupils. The Examples have been almost entirely taken from the Woolwich Papers.

The Second Part, comprising the Elements of Descriptive Geometry to the extent required for admission to the Royal Military Academy, Woolwich, will shortly be ready for the press.

WOODFORD, N.E.
November 1859.

CONTENTS.

PRACTICAL PLANE GEOMETRY.

INTRODUCTORY REMARKS.

THE following hints will be found serviceable to a beginner in Geometrical Drawing.

THE PAPER, of good quality but not too highly glazed, should be made to present as smooth a surface as possible.

INDIAN RUBBER must be used sparingly and with great care on a drawing, previous to its being inked in.

THE PENCIL, either an HH or an HHH, should not be excessively hard. In drawing a line, let the pencil be gently pressed upon the paper, and slightly inclined in the direction in which the line is being drawn; care being taken to keep it, throughout the operation, in the same position with reference to the plane of the paper.

INDIAN INK, free from grit, and carefully rubbed down with water, is to be used.

THE DRAWING PEN must be held in a manner similar to that directed for the pencil, both nibs being equally pressed upon the paper. Before the pen is used, the ends of the blades should be moistened on the inside with clean water. Previously to its being laid aside it ought to be carefully cleaned and dried. The ink can be conveniently introduced by means of a narrow slip of paper.

B

CARE OF INSTRUMENTS.—Neatness and accuracy of construction are essential requisites in this kind of drawing; consequently, too great care cannot be taken of the instruments. The points of compasses and the edges of rulers must be scrupulously guarded from injury: for it is impossible, with pointless dividers and a notched ruler, to attain even an approach to accuracy.

THICKNESS OF LINES. — In constructing problems, it will be advisable to draw the given lines thin and continuous, the lines of construction thin and dotted; those lines, the determination of which is the object of the problem, thick and continuous.

THE POSITION OF A POINT will be more accurately determined by the intersection of two lines, the more nearly the angle, at which these lines cut each other, approaches to a right angle; this angle should never be less than 20°.

Instead of using the pen or pencil sweeps, to find a point, by the intersection of a circle with another line, the hair dividers may with great advantage be employed for that purpose.

LINES THROUGH POINTS.—Before drawing a line with the aid of a ruler, it should be carefully ascertained that the ruler is placed in such a position that the point of the pen or pencil will pass exactly through the point or points through which the line is to be drawn.

In describing circles care must be taken to prevent the leg of the compasses, at the centre, from making a hole in the paper; otherwise, the exactness of construction desired will not be attained. This should be particularly attended to in drawing concentric circles and circles of large radii.

These remarks would extend to considerable length if made to embrace a description of the various instruments employed in drawing. This was deemed unnecessary, inasmuch as all requisite information on that subject may be found in a Treatise on Mathematical Instruments, published in Weale's Shilling Series. A short explanation, however, of the use of the *sector*, the *protractor*, and the *marquois scales*, has been introduced.

CHAPTER I.

PRACTICAL PLANE GEOMETRY.

PROBLEM I.

To bisect a rectilineal angle.

Let M A N (Pl. I. Fig. 1) be the given angle.

With A as a centre, and a radius less than A M or A N, describe a circle cutting these lines in B and C.

With B and C as centres, and a radius greater than half the distance from B to C, describe two circles intersecting in D. Join A D.

A D will bisect the angle M A N.

To prove this, join B D, C D, and apply *Euc.* I. 8.

Obs. In Euclid's construction of this problem, the triangle B D C is equilateral, only because he has not previously shown how to construct an isosceles triangle.

PROBLEM II.

At a point in a straight line, to make an angle equal to a given rectilineal angle.

Let M A N (Pl. I. Fig. 2) be the given angle, P the point in the line P Q.

With A as a centre, and a radius less than A M or A N, describe a circle cutting these lines in B and C.

With P as a centre, and a radius P Q equal to A B, describe the circle Q R.

With the dividers set off Q R equal to B C. Join P R.

The angle Q P R will be equal to the angle M A N.

For the arc Q R is equal to the arc C B, and (*Euc.* III. 27) in equal circles the angles which stand upon equal circumferences are equal to one another.

Obs. If the straight lines C B, Q R be drawn, the equality of the angles M A N, Q P R may be proved by *Euc.* I. 8. The construction, however, is somewhat simpler than that in *Euc.* I. 23.

PROBLEM III.

Through a point to draw a straight line parallel to a given straight line.

Let M N (Pl. I. Fig. 3) be the given line, P the point.

With P as a centre describe a circle, cutting M N in A.

With A as a centre, and a radius A P, describe a circle cutting M N in Q.

With the dividers make A R equal to P Q.

The straight line drawn through P and R will be parallel to M N (*Euc.* III. 27, and I. 27).

PROBLEM IV.

To divide a straight line into n equal parts; n being a power of 2.

Let M N (Pl. I. Fig. 4) be the given line.

1. Let $n = 2$. With M and N as centres, and a radius greater than $\frac{1}{2}$ M N, describe two circles intersecting in A and B.

Join A B; if A B cut M N in a, a will be the point of bisection of M N (*Euc.* I. 8 and 4).

2. If $n = 4$, bisect a N in b by a construction similar to that in the preceding case.

b N will be $\frac{1}{4}$ of M N.

By repeating this process with b N, $\frac{1}{8}$ of M N is obtained, as c N; and by the same method $\frac{1}{16}$, $\frac{1}{32}$, $\frac{1}{64}$, &c., of the line M N may be found.

Having in this way determined $\frac{1}{n}$th part of a line, the line may be divided into n equal parts by setting off this length along it with the hair dividers. This operation, however, requires great care; therefore, in cases where accuracy is desired, it will be better to find each point by a separate construction.

PROBLEM V.

To draw a straight line, from a given point, perpendicular to a given straight line.

Let P be the given point, M N the line.

1. Let P (Pl. I. Fig. 5) be without and not near the end of M N.

With P as a centre describe a circle, cutting M N in A and B.

With A and B as centres, and a radius greater than $\frac{1}{2}$ A B, describe two circles intersecting in C.

Join P C; let it cut M N in Q.

P Q is the perpendicular required (*Euc.* I. 8, 4, and Def. 10).

2. Let P (Pl. I. Fig. 6) be in, and not near the end of, M N. Make P A equal to P B. With A and B as centres, and a radius greater than $\frac{1}{2}$ A B, describe two circles cutting in Q.

Join P Q; P Q will be the perpendicular required (*Euc.* I. 8).

3. Let P be without, and near the end of, M N (Pl. I. Fig. 7). In M N take a point A; join P A; if P A be not perpendicular to M N, upon P A describe a circle, cutting M N in Q.

Join P Q; P Q will be perpendicular to M N (*Euc.* III. 31).

4. Let P be in, and near the end of, M N (Pl. I. Fig. 8). Take a point C not in M N : join P C; if P C be not perpendicular to M N, with C as a centre, and radius C P, describe a circle cutting M N in A ; draw the diameter A Q.

Join Q P; P Q will be perpendicular to M N (*Euc.* III. 31).

Obs. The fourth case may be solved by the following construction :—

With P (Pl. I. Fig. 9) as a centre, and a radius of 4 equal parts, describe a circle cutting M N in A; and a second circle with a radius of 3 equal parts, from the same scale.

With centre A and a radius of 5 such equal parts, describe a third circle cutting the second in Q.

Join P Q; P Q will be perpendicular to M N (*Euc.* I. 48). For $3^2 + 4^2 = 5^2$.

N.B. This method is often employed in the field when no instrument for measuring angles is at hand.

Ex. Let it be required to start from the station P, on the lineMN, in a direction at right angles to M N.

Measure the distance P A 8 feet, and the distances Q A, Q P, 10 and 6 feet respectively.

P Q will be perpendicular to M N, and is, therefore, the direction required.

It is evident that any other unit of length might have been used instead of feet ; also that the sides of the triangle might have been any numbers which are to one another as 3, 4, 5.

PROBLEM VI.

To divide a straight line into n equal parts; n being any number whatever.

Let M N (Pl. I. Fig. 10) be the given line, and $n=13$. From M draw an indefinite straight line M A, perpendicular to M N.

With N as a centre, and a radius of thirteen equal parts, taken from a scale, and such that their sum is greater than M N, describe a circle cutting M A in A.

Join N A, and divide it into thirteen equal parts, by setting off along it from one end one of the equal parts taken from the scale.

Through the points of division g_1, g_2, g_3, g_4, &c. &c., draw $g_1 p_1$, $g_2 p_2, g_3 p_3, g_4 p_4$, &c., &c., parallel to M A. M N will be divided in the points p_1, p_2, p_3, p_4, &c., similarly to N A; but N A is divided into thirteen equal parts, therefore M N is also divided into thirteen equal parts.

Obs. M A might have been drawn to make any angle with M N ; but, as was observed in the Introductory Remarks, a point is more accurately determined when two lines intersect at right angles than when they cut each other at any oblique angle.

Cor. It is evident that any aliquot part of a straight line may be found by this problem.

Solution 2. To find any fraction of a given straight line.

Let M N (Pl. I. Fig. 11) be the given line, and $n=7$ the denominator of the fraction.

Draw M A perpendicular to M N; with N as a centre, and a
radius of seven equal parts, describe a circle cutting M A in p_7.

Complete the rectangle Mp_7g_7N; divide Np_7 into seven equal
parts, in p_1, p_2, p_3, p_4, &c. &c.

Draw p_1g_1, p_2g_2, p_3g_3, p_4g_4, &c. &c., parallel to M N, or
p_7g_7.

Then by similar triangles—

$$N p_1 : N p_7 :: p_1 g_1 : p_7 g_7;$$

but $Np_1=\frac{1}{7}$ of Np_7; therefore $p_1 g_1=\frac{1}{7}$ of $p_7 g_7=\frac{1}{7}$ of M N;
similarly it may be shown that $p_2g_2=\frac{2}{7}$ of M N, $p_3g_3=\frac{3}{7}$ of
M N, &c. &c.

Obs. This will be applied in the construction of diagonal scales.

PROBLEM VII.

To draw circles, of given radii, to touch each other.

Draw an indefinite straight line M N (Pl. II. Fig. 1); in it take
a point P, as the point of contact.

Make P A, P D equal to the given radii.

With A and D as centres, P A, P D as radii, describe the
circles Q P, S P. These circles will touch each other in P
(*Euc.* III. 11 and 12).

In the same manner circles P V and P R may be described
with C and B as centres, C P and B P as radii, touching each
other, and M Q P, S P V, in the point P.

For all circles which pass through P, and have their centres in
M N, touch each other.

PROBLEM VIII.

To draw a tangent to a given circle from a point either without or in the circumference.

1. Let the point P (Pl. II. Fig. 2) be without the circle Q C R.
Find S, the centre of the circle (*Euc.* III. 1).

Join P S, upon it describe the semicircle P R S, cutting

Q C R in R. Join P R; P R T will be the tangent required (*Euc.* III. 31 and 16).

2. Let the point Q (Pl. II. Fig. 2) be in the circumference. Find the centre S, join Q S.

Through Q draw A Q B perpendicular to Q S by Prob. V. case 4, A Q B will be a tangent (*Euc.* III. 16 cor.)

Cor. A circle may be described to touch a given straight line, as A B (Pl. II. Fig. 2) in a given point Q, by drawing from Q, Q S perpendicular to A B, making Q S equal to the radius of the required circle, and with centre S, radius S Q describing the circle Q C R. (*Euc.* III. 16).

PROBLEM IX.

· To describe a circle passing through three given points, not in the same straight line.

Let P, Q, R (Pl. II. Fig. 3) be the given points.

Join P Q, Q R, bisect the lines P Q, Q R in A B.

Draw A C, B C perpendicular to P Q, Q R respectively, and intersecting in C.

The point C will be equidistant from P, Q, and R (*Euc.* IV. 5), and is consequently the centre of the circle P Q R, passing through the points P, Q, R (*Euc.* III. 9).

PROBLEM X.

Upon a straight line to describe a segment of a circle which shall contain a given angle.

Let M N (Pl. II. Fig. 4) be the given line, B the angle.

1. If B be a right angle, upon M N describe the semicircle M P N (Pl. II. Fig. 4).

The angle in the segment M P N will be a right angle, and therefore equal to B.

2. If B (Pl. II. Fig. 5) be not a right angle.

· At the points M and N, in the line M N, make the angles N M D, M N C each equal to B.

Draw M N and N A perpendicular to M D and N D respectively, intersecting in A, M A will be equal to N A (*Euc.* I. 6).

With A as a centre, and a radius A M, or A N, describe the circle M Q P N; the angle in the segment M Q N, or that in the segment M P N, will be equal to B (*Euc.* III. 32), according as B is greater or less than a right angle.

Through equidistant points in a straight line, to draw parallel lines at a given distance apart.

Let M N (Pl. II. Fig. 6) be the line, p_1, p_2, p_3, p_4, p_5, p_6, points in it, situated so that $p_1 p_2 = p_2 p_3 = p_3 p_4 = p_4 p_5 = p_5 p_6$, and let d be the given distance.

With p_6 as a centre and a radius equal to six times d, describe a circle.

From p_1 draw $p_1 a_6$ to touch this circle in a_6 (Prob. VIII). Join $p_6 a_6$.

Through p_2, p_3, p_4, p_5, draw the lines $p_2 a_2$, $p_3 a_3$, $p_4 a_4$, $p_5 a_5$, parallel to $p_6 a_6$; these will be the lines required.

For it is evident that they are all perpendicular to $p_1 a_6$, and that

$$p_1 a_2 = a_2 a_3 = a_3 a_4 = a_4 a_5 = a_5 a_6 = \tfrac{1}{6} \text{ of } p_1 a_6 = d.$$

* *Cor.* The given distance d can never be greater than the distance between two of the given points.

To find a fourth proportional to three given straight lines.

Let A, B, C, (Pl. II. Fig. 7) be the lines.

Draw Q P, Q R containing an angle R, about half a right angle.

Make Q D equal to A; D E equal to B; Q F equal to C. Join D F.

Through E draw E G parallel to D F, and cutting Q R in G.

F G will be the fourth proportional required (*Euc.* VI. 2).

· *Cor.* To find a third proportional to A and B (Pl. II. Fig. 8), make Q C equal to A; Q E equal to C D, equal to B, and construct as before.

E F will be the line required.

PROBLEM XIII.

To find a mean proportional between two given lines.

Let A B (Pl. II. Fig. 9) be the lines.

Draw an indefinite straight line M N; in it take a point P.

Make P D equal to A, P E equal to B.

Upon D E, describe the semicircle D Q E.

Draw P Q perpendicular to M N, and meeting the circumference in Q.

P Q will be the line required (*Euc.* VI. 8).

PROBLEM XIV.

To divide a straight line similarly to a given divided line.

Let M N (Pl. II. Fig. 10) be the line divided into any number of parts in p_1, p_2, p_3, p_4, &c. &c.

P Q the line to be divided.

Draw M N parallel to P Q, at a convenient distance from it.

Join M P, N Q; if M N be equal to P Q, M P will be parallel to N Q.

Draw $p_1 a_1$, $p_2 a_2$, $p_3 a_3$, $p_4 a_4$, &c. &c., parallel to M P. Then P Q will be divided in the points a_1, a_2, a_3, a_4, &c. &c.; similarly to M N (*Euc.* I. 34).

If M P be not parallel to N Q (Pl. II. Fig. 11), let them meet in A. Join $A p_1$, $A p_2$, $A p_3$, $A p_4$, &c. &c., cutting P Q in the points a_1, a_2, a_3, a_4, &c. &c. Then P Q will be divided in these points similarly to M N (*Euc.* VI. 2).

PROBLEM XV.

To describe a square upon a given straight line.

Let A B (Pl. I. Fig. 12) be the line.

Draw A E at right angles to A B; make A F equal to A B; through F and B draw F D and B D respectively parallel to B A and A F.

A F D B will be the square required (*Euc.* i. 46).

PROBLEM XVI.

To describe a parallelogram equal to a given triangle, and having an angle equal to a given angle.

Let P Q R (Pl. II. Fig. 12) be the given triangle. Bisect any side Q R in S. Make the angle R S A equal to the given angle.

Through R draw R B parallel to S A; through P draw P A B parallel to Q R

A B R S will be the parallelogram required (*Euc.* i. 41).

PROBLEM XVII.

To divide a straight line in extreme and mean ratio.

Let M N (Pl. II. Fig. 13) be the line.

Through M draw A C perpendicular to M N.

Make M A equal to ½ M N; A C equal to A N; M P equal to M C.

M N will be divided in the point P, so that N M : M P :: M P : P N (*Euc.* II. 11; VI. 17).

PROBLEM XVIII.

Given, the area of a square to find its side; or to construct a square of given area.

(Pl. II. Fig. 14.) Let the area of the square be n superficia units.

In any straight line M N; take M P equal to n lineal units; P N equal to one lineal unit.

Upon M N describe a semicircle.

Draw P Q at right angles to M N and meeting the circumference in Q.

P Q will be the side required : —

for $P Q^2 = M P \times P N = n \times 1 = n.$

Obs. This construction is useful when n is not a square number, and it is required to find the side of the square accurately.

N.B. This problem may also be solved by *Euc.* III. 36.

PROBLEM XIX.

Upon a given line, to describe a rectilineal figure similar to a given rectilineal figure.

Let A B C D E F (Pl. III. Fig. 2) be the given figure; *a b* the given line.

Join A C, A D, A E.

At the points *a* and *b* in the line *a b* make the angles *b a c*, *a b c*, equal to B A C, A B C, respectively; at *a* and *c* in *a c*, make the angles *c a d*, *a c d*, equal to C A D, A C D; at *a* and *d* in *a d*,

make the angles *e a d*, *a d e*, equal to E A D, A D E; at *a* and *e* in *a e*,

make the angles *e a f*, *a e f*, equal to E A F, A E F:

the figure *a b c d e f* will be similar to the figure A B C D E F.

Cor. Fig. A B C D E F : fig. *a b c d e f* :: A B² : *a b²* (*Euc.* VI. 20).

If, therefore, *a b c d e f* is required to be $\frac{1}{n}$ of A B C D E F,

A B² will be equal to *a b²* × *n*, and *a b* equal to $\frac{A B}{\sqrt{n}}$. This shows how to describe a rectilineal figure which shall be any multiple of, and similar to, a given rectilineal figure.

PROBLEM XX.

To reduce a rectilineal figure of *n* sides to a figure having a number of sides less than *n*.

Let the given figure A B C D E F G (Pl. III. Fig. 1) have seven sides.

Join F A; through G draw G R parallel to F A.

Join F R; then (*Euc.* I. 37) the triangle F R A is equal to the triangle F G A.

The triangle F O A is common to both of these triangles.

Therefore the triangle F O G is equal to the triangle R O A. From the figure A B C D E F take the triangle F O G: to the remainder add the triangle R O A; and the resulting figure, B C D E F R, will evidently be equal to the original figure, A B C D E F G, which has thus been reduced to an equivalent figure of six sides.

Join E R; through F draw F P parallel to E R.

Join E P; the figure B C D E P, of five sides, will be equal to the figure B C D E F R, and therefore equivalent to the figure A B C D E F G.

Join D B; through C draw C S parallel to D B; join D S; the figure S D E P, of four sides, will be equal to A B C D E F G.

Join E S; through D draw D Q parallel to E S.

Join E Q; the triangle E P Q will be equivalent to the original figure.

The proof in each step of the reduction is similar to that in the first.

. *Obs.* This problem is of frequent occurrence when an irregular polygon of any number of sides has to be reduced to an equivalent triangle, for the purpose of calculating its area.

Ex. Draw E a perpendicular to P Q; then

the area of the triangle E P Q = $\frac{1}{2}$ E a × P Q :

if, therefore, E a, P Q, be measured by means of a scale, the area may immediately be found.

EXAMPLES FOR PRACTICE.

1. From one extremity of a line three inches long draw a perpendicular two inches long without producing the line. Base the construction on geometrical principles.

2. Find, by construction, a mean proportional between two lines 2·4 and 3·8 inches long respectively.

3. A line 5 inches long is divided into six equal parts: draw parallel lines half an inch apart through the divisions of the given line.

4. Construct a square of 5·36 inches area by two different processes without extracting the square root of 5·36.

5. Construct a square of which the area shall be equal to the sum of four squares having their sides ·5, ·75, ·875, and 1·125 inches respectively.

6. Divide a line 3 inches long into seven equal parts, by three methods.

7. Bisect an angle whose angular point falls without the limit of the paper.

8. Make a triangle of which the sides are 3·5, 1·75, and 2 inches respectively.

9. Describe a rectangle of which the sides are 3·45 and 2·65 inches. Find its area.

10. Divide a line 3 inches long into 7½ equal parts.

11. Find a line which shall have the same ratio to a line 1·5 inches long that 3 inches has to 1·75 inches.

12. Given a circle, or an arc of a circle, to find its centre.

N.B. Draw two chords, not parallel to one another; from the points of bisection of these chords draw perpendiculars to them. The point in which these perpendiculars cut each other will be the centre. (*Euc.* III. 1. cor.)

13. Trisect a right angle.

14. Describe upon a given line, as a base, an isosceles triangle, having a given vertical angle.

15. Draw parallel lines, one inch apart, through points in a straight line, at distances of two inches.

16. Draw a circle circumscribing a triangle, of which the sides are respectively 4, 5, and 6 inches.

17. Construct a square equal to a triangle, of which the sides are respectively 1·5, 2, and 2·25 inches.

18. A B is a straight line 2 inches long; find, with the com-

passes only, a point P in continuation of A B, on the side of B, and 2 inches from it.

19. Reduce an irregular figure of five sides to an equivalent triangle, and calculate the area.

20. In the triangle A B C, A B = 150 yards, B C = 180 yards, A C = 250 yards. Find by construction a point P, when the angles A P B and C P B are respectively 37° 45′ and 52° 30′.

CHAP. II.

ON THE USE OF THE SECTOR, THE PROTRACTOR, AND THE MARQUOIS SCALES.

Definition. The SECTOR is an instrument formed of two flat rulers or legs of equal length fixed to a common centre, and movable about that centre in a plane.

Def. SECTORAL LINES are lines drawn in pairs from the centre, one of each pair on either leg. The most important of these are the line of lines, marked L; the line of chords, marked C; and the line of polygons, marked Pol.

Instead of a single line, for a sectoral line, on each leg three parallel lines are drawn, to facilitate the division of the line into equal parts for use. In all cases the points of the dividers must be applied to the innermost of these, — that is, to the one which radiates from the centre.

Def. A LATERAL DISTANCE is a distance measured from the centre along any sectoral line.

Def. A TRANSVERSE DISTANCE is a distance measured from a point in one line of a pair to the corresponding point in the other line.

Explanation of the principle of the LINE OF LINES.

Let P (Pl. III. Fig. 3) be the centre, P L, P L', the line of lines, divided into ten equal parts in the points 1, 2, 3, 4, 5, 6, 7, 8, 9 (in the sector constructed for use each of these primary divisions is divided into ten equal secondary divisions, so that the line of lines is divided into 100 equal parts): draw L L', $l\, l'$; then because $P\,l' = P\,l$ and $P\,L' = P\,L,$

$\qquad$ L L' is parallel to $l\, l'$, and consequently

$$l\, l' : L\,L' :: P\,l' : P\,L';$$

therefore whatever part $p\,l'$ is of $P\,L'$, $l\,l'$ is the same part of $L\,L'$.

1. Let it be required to bisect a given straight line.

Open the sector until the transverse distance at 10 is equal to the given line; then the transverse distance at 5 will be equal to one half of the line.

N.B. The transverse distances at 8 and 4, 6 and 3, or 4 and 2, might have been employed for the bisection.

2. To divide a straight line into any number of equal parts.

Let the required number of parts be 9.

Make the transverse distance at 9 equal to the given line; then the transverse distance at 1 will be equal to $\frac{1}{9}$ of the line.

This construction may be effected more accurately by making the transverse distance at 9 equal to the given line, as before, and then setting off from each end of the line the transverse distance at 4. The line will thus be divided into three parts, the middle one of which will be $\frac{1}{9}$ of the line, each of the others $\frac{4}{9}$ of it.

Cor. This shows how from a given line to cut off any aliquot part.

3. To find any fraction of a given line.

Ex. 1. $\frac{3}{5}$ of a line 4·25 inches long.

Make the transverse distance at 5 equal to the line, the transverse distance at 3 will be $\frac{3}{5}$ of the line.

Ex. 2. To find $\frac{9}{23}$ of a line 5·17 inches long.

Since there are only ten primary divisions, recourse must be had to the secondary divisions, to solve this problem. In order to bring the construction some distance from the centre, which will increase the accuracy of the result, multiply the numerator and the denominator of the fraction by some number which will not make the denominator when so multiplied greater than 100 ; in this case 4 will be a convenient multiplier ; then $\frac{9}{23} = \frac{36}{92}$; make the transverse distance at the secondary division 92 equal to 5·17 inches, the transverse distance at the 36th secondary division will be $\frac{36}{92}$, that is $\frac{9}{23}$ of 5·17 inches, as required.

4. To find a fourth proportional to three given straight lines.

Let A, B, C be the lines, make the transverse distance at the lateral distance A equal to B, then the transverse distance at the lateral distance C will be the fourth proportional required.

Cor. If a third proportional to A and B had been required, the solution would have been performed in a similar way, for in this case B = C, and therefore the transverse distance at the lateral distance B must have been taken.

N.B. In a correctly divided sector the line of lines will be found a convenient instrument for solving Problems IV., VI., XII., and XIII. of the Practical Geometry.

THE LINE OF CHORDS.

The line of chords is chiefly used for setting off angles of a given number of degrees. It is so constructed that if the sector be opened until the transverse distance at 60 is equal to the chord of 60° in any circle, the transverse distance at any other number on the line of chords will be equal to the chord of that number of degrees in the same circle. For example, the transverse distance marked 23 will be the chord of 23°.

Ex. 1. To set off an angle of 35° (Pl. IV. Fig. 1).

With the point M, in the straight line M N as a centre, and any radius M P, less than M N, describe a circle P T.

Make the transverse distance at 60 equal to M·P, because the chord of 60° is equal to the radius.

With the hair dividers make P Q equal to the transverse distance at 35, join M Q.

The angle N M Q will be the angle required.

Ex. 2. To set off an angle greater than 60° but less than 90°.

Let the angle be 75°.

From M (Pl. IV. Fig. 2) draw M Q at right angles to M N.

By the preceding example make the angle Q M R equal to 15°; the angle R M N is the angle required for 90° — 15° = 75°.

Ex. 3. To make an angle greater than 90°.

Let the angle be 133°.

Draw M Q (Pl. IV. Fig. 3) at right angles to M N; make the angle Q M S equal to 43°.

The angle N M S is the angle required for 90° + 43° = 133°.

Examples 2 and 3 might have been solved by making an angle equal to $\frac{1}{2}$ or $\frac{1}{3}$ of the required angle, and setting this off along the arc as many times as necessary. But since this method sometimes gives rise to fractions of degrees, it will generally be found more convenient to adopt the constructions in the text.

Cor. It is evident that an angle of a given number of degrees may be readily divided into 2, 3, 4, 5, &c. equal parts by means of the line of chords.

THE LINE OF POLYGONS.

This line is chiefly used for the purpose of dividing the circumferences of circles into equal parts, to describe regular polygons. It is constructed in such a manner that if the sector be opened until the transverse distance at 6 is equal to the radius of any circle, that is, the side of a regular hexagon (*Euc.* IV. 14) inscribed in that circle, the transverse distances at 5, 7, 8, 9, 10, 11, 12 will be respectively equal to the sides of a regular pentagon, heptagon, octagon, &c. &c. inscribed in the same circle.

Ex. 1. To inscribe a heptagon in a given circle.

Let S (Pl. IV. Fig. 4) be the centre of the circle A D F; S A its radius.

Open the sector until the transverse distance at 6 is equal to
S A; then the transverse distance at 7 will be equal to the side
of the heptagon.

Let A B be this distance: place around in the circle straight
lines B C, C D, D E, E F, F G, G A, each equal to B A.

The figure A B C D E F G will be the heptagon required.

Ex. 2. To describe a regular nonagon upon a given
straight line.

Let A B (Pl. IV. Fig. 5) be the given line.

Open the sector until the transverse distance at 9 is equal to
A B. With A and B as centres, and a radius equal to the
transverse distance at 6, describe two circles intersecting in S.

With S as a centre, and the same radius as before, describe the circle A B C L. Place around in it the straight
lines B C, C D, D E, E F, &c. &c. each equal to A B:
A B C D E F G H K will be a regular nonagon.

Obs. If A be the number of degrees in an angle of a regular polygon of
n sides, $A° = 180° - \dfrac{360°}{n}$ (*Euc.* I. 32, Cor. 1), consequently when $\dfrac{360°}{n}$ is
an integer, a regular polygon may be described upon a given straight line
by the following method :—

Ex. Let $n = 8$, therefore $A° = 180° - 45° = 135°$;
let A B (Fig. 6, Pl. IV.) be the given line.

Make the angle A B P equal to 135°. Take B C equal to A B; describe
the circle A C E G H, passing through the points A B C; place around in
this circle the lines C D, D E, E F, F G, G H, each equal to A B or B C.
The figure A B C D E F G H will be a regular octagon.

THE MARQUOIS SCALES.

A set of these consists of two rectangular rulers and a right-
angled triangle. Each ruler has two natural and two artificial
scales engraved on each side of it, with figures in the middle of
the former to denote the number of parts into which the inch is
divided. The scales given are those of 30, 60, 25, 50 parts to
an inch on one ruler, and 20, 40, 35, 45 on the other: from which
can also be obtained those of 1, 2, 3, 4, 5, 6, 7, 8, 9, 10, 12, and

15, making in all twenty scales. The natural scales are divided in the ordinary manner, the left-hand primary division being subdivided into ten parts; but the artificial scale has all the primary divisions, each of which is equal to three of those of the natural scale adjoining, subdivided into tenths, each of which is therefore equal to three of the natural subdivisions, and it has the zero point in the middle of the scale. The divisions are numbered both ways. The longest side of the triangle is three times the shortest side, and has a short line drawn perpendicular to it at the middle.

Let A B (Pl. III. Fig. 5) be the edge of the ruler, P Q R the first position of the triangle, p q r the position into which it has been moved.

Draw p s parallel to Q R, then by similar triangles —

$$P\,p : p\,s :: P\,R : R\,Q;$$

but P R is three times R Q, therefore P p is three times p s. In order, therefore, to draw parallel lines at given distances apart, place the star line on the triangle, against one of the divisions on the artificial scale, and, holding the ruler firmly in its place, slip the triangle along as many divisions as the given distance occupies in the natural scale. It will be found that its bevelled edge has moved in a direction perpendicular to itself, through the required distance or one-third of that travelled by the star line along the ruler.

THE PROTRACTOR.

This instrument is used for the purpose of protracting or laying down angles of a given number of degrees by the method of coincidence. The construction of it is indicated in Pl. III. Fig. 4.

Ex. Let it be required to make an angle of 40° at the point P, in the line M N; with the centre on P, move the protractor until the line radiating from the centre, and marked 40°, coincides with M N; draw P Q along the edge, the angle Q P M will be the angle required.

If the given line be P Q, and not long enough to admit of

applying the instrument in this manner, place the centre on P, as before, then with a very finely pointed pencil, or with the hair dividers, mark a point on the paper, where the radiating line through 40° meets the edge. Remove the protractor, and draw the line M N through P and the point thus found. M P Q will be the angle.

EXAMPLES FOR PRACTICE.

1. The area of a triangle is 4·6 square inches, one of its angles is 50°, another is 65°. Construct the triangle.

Note. In this example simple multiplication is the only arithmetical process allowed.

2. Two straight lines intersect at an angle of 35°; draw a circle of 2·25 inches radius touching both lines.

3. Inscribe an octagon in a square, the side of the square being 2·43 inches.

4. Construct a regular heptagon with a side of 2 inches. Explain the mode of construction.

5. One side of a triangle is 2·7 inches long, the opposite angle B is 65°, $\dfrac{b}{\text{sec. A}}$ is 1·6 inches long. Construct the triangle.

6. Construct a triangle, two of whose sides are 2·75 and 3·2 inches long respectively, the included angle 65°. Describe a circle about the triangle, showing how the centre is found.

7. Describe two circles with radii of two inches and one inch respectively, tangent to one another.
Inscribe a nonagon in the first.

8. On a base of 3 inches describe an irregular figure of seven sides; reduce it to a triangle of equivalent area, and calculate that area.

9. Explain the principle of the line of lines on the sector, and from a line 4·37 inches long, cut off portions respectively equal to $\frac{3}{17}$ and $\frac{4}{19}$ of its length.

10. Draw an arc of 73° with a radius of 3·36 inches, and one of 100° touching the former at one extremity, radius 2·5 inches.

11. By means of the line of chords on the sector draw an angle of 102°, and an arc of 2·25 inches radius, touching both lines of the angle. Mark the points of contact of the arc and the straight lines.

12. Draw arcs of radii 2 and 3 inches respectively, with their centres 6 inches apart, and a third arc 2·5 inches to touch the other two externally.

13. Divide a line 4·13 inches long, so that the parts may be as 3, 7, 2, 17, 4½.

14. Draw a line two inches long perpendicular to a given line 3 inches long, from a point ¾ of an inch from one end, by geometrical construction.

15. Construct an isosceles triangle equal in area to the sum of four squares, of which the sides are respectively ½, ⅝, ⅞, and 1¼ inch.

16. From a circle of 1½ inch radius cut off two segments containing angles of 32° and 94° respectively.

17. Make an angle of 75°, bisect it with the compasses and ruler alone, and describe a circle of 1 inch radius tangential to both lines containing the angle.

18. Draw six parallel dotted lines of equal thickness, each 3·14 inches long, and at equal distances of $\frac{5}{18}$ inch.

19. Describe a segment of a circle having a base of 2·36 inches, and containing an angle of 115°.

20. Construct a regular octagon, with a side 1·78 inch; reduce the figure to an equivalent triangle.

21. A right-angled triangle has a base of 2 inches and an area of 3 square inches; construct it, and also one similar to it of half its area.

CHAP. III.

SCALES.

WHEN an object to be represented on paper is of such magnitude that it would be either inconvenient or impossible to make a full size drawing of it, the usual practice is to construct a drawing of which each line has a known and fixed ratio to the line which it represents.

In order that such a drawing may be generally intelligible, draughtsmen employ two methods, by either of which the absolute length of any line in the original may at once be determined from the draught.

The first method is to attach to the drawing a fraction called the REPRESENTATIVE FRACTION, which expresses the ratio above mentioned.

Thus the fraction $\frac{1}{24}$ attached to a plan would show that 1 inch on such plan represented 24 inches; $\frac{1}{2}$ an inch, 12 inches. In short, that the distance between any two points in the drawing was $\frac{1}{24}$ of the distance between the points corresponding to them in the original.

By the second method, in addition to the representative fraction, a graduated straight line, termed a Scale, is annexed to the drawing, for the purpose of conveniently measuring distances. The unit of length in this scale must evidently bear the same ratio to the real unit of length that a line in the drawing bears to the line which it represents. Thus, if the representative fraction were $\frac{1}{60}$, 1 inch on the scale would represent 5 feet.

It should be observed that these scales are usually, though not necessarily, constructed of such a length as to represent a distance which is a multiple of ten lineal units of some kind; as 80 miles, 50 yards, 100 toises, 500 versts.

The construction of these scales, called PLAIN SCALES, will be best illustrated by examples, of which several are subjoined.

1. To construct a scale of $\frac{1}{24}$, or 2 feet to an inch.

The number of feet to be represented by the scale may be assumed at pleasure; in this case let it be 12·5 feet, and put x for the number of inches which will represent that distance: then —

$$\text{ft.} \quad \text{ft.}$$
$$24 : 12\cdot5 :: 12 : x,$$

whence $x = \dfrac{12 \times 12\cdot5}{24} = 6\cdot25 =$ the number of inches required.

For, by the question, 24 feet are represented by 1 foot, or 12 inches, and 24 feet evidently has the same ratio to 12·5 feet, that 1 foot ($= 12$ inches) has to the number of inches which will represent 12·5 feet.

Construction. (Pl. IV. Fig. 7) Draw, in pencil, three straight lines, rather more than $6\frac{1}{4}$ inches long, parallel to one another, and $\frac{4}{80}$ of an inch apart. On the lowest of these measure off a distance of 6·25 inches, and divide this distance into 5 equal parts, each of these will represent 2·5 feet, that is, 10 quarter-feet. Subdivide the left-hand primary division into 10 equal parts, to show single quarter-feet. Through each of the primary divisions draw perpendiculars from the lowest of the three lines to the uppermost. Through the secondary divisions draw perpendiculars to the middle line, and to half-way between the middle and upper lines alternately, as shown in the diagram. Ink in these lines, and the middle one of the three lightly, the bottom one rather heavily, the top one not at all; commencing from the left number the secondary divisions 8, 6, 4, 2, 0; the primary ones, 10, 20, 30, 40; opposite the last number write the words quarter-feet, and the scale is completed.

2. To construct a scale of 2 miles to an inch (Pl. IV. Fig. 9).

Let the scale represent 11 miles: then—

$$\text{miles.} \quad \text{miles.} \quad \text{in.} \quad \text{in.}$$
$$2 : 11 :: 1 : 5\cdot5 = \text{the length of the scale.}$$

Divide a line 5·5 inches long into 11 equal parts, each of these will represent a mile. Subdivide the first of these into 8 equal parts, to show furlongs. Complete the scale as shown in the figure.

$$\text{Representative fraction} = \frac{1}{2 \times 1760 \times 36} = \frac{1}{126720}.$$

3. To construct a scale of 12 feet to ·875 inch (Pl: IV. Fig. 11).

Let the scale represent 60 feet : then —

$$\begin{array}{cccc} \text{ft.} & \text{ft.} & \text{in.} & \text{in.} \\ 12 & : 60 & :: ·875 & : 4·375 \end{array}$$

Divide a line 4·375 inches long into 6 equal parts, to show tens of feet, and the first of these into ten equal parts to show feet.

$$\text{Representative fraction} = \frac{·875}{144} = \frac{7}{1152}.$$

4. The representative fractions of two plans of a Russian fort are $\frac{1}{800}$ and $\frac{1}{1260}$: construct a scale of French toises for the former and one of Russian archines for the latter.

(1 toise = 2·13142 English yards.)
(1 archine = ·7777 English yards.)

(i.) To make a scale of toises $\frac{1}{800}$, 80 toises long.

$$\begin{array}{ccc} \text{toises.} & \text{toises.} & \text{toise.} \\ 800 & : 80 & :: 1 \end{array} : \text{length of scale in toises.}$$

$$= \frac{\overset{\text{English inches.}}{2·13142 \times 36 \times 80}}{800} \overset{\text{inches.}}{= 7·673112.}$$

Divide a line 7·673 inches long into 8 equal parts, to show tens of toises; subdivide the first primary division into ten equal parts, to show toises.

(ii.) To make a scale of archines $\frac{1}{1260}$, 300 archines long.

$$\begin{array}{ccc} \text{ar.} & \text{ar.} & \text{ar.} \\ 1260 & : 300 & :: 1 \end{array} : \text{length of scale in archines.}$$

$$\therefore \text{length} = \frac{\overset{\text{English inches.}}{·7777 \times 36 \times 300}}{1260} \overset{\text{in.}}{=} \overset{\text{in.}}{6·666} = 6·67 \text{ nearly.}$$

Divide a line 6·67 inches long into 15 equal parts, each of which will show 20 archines: subdivide the first of these into 4 equal parts, each of which will show 5 archines.

Obs. The length of these scales is optional. Every scale should, however, be sufficiently long to allow any lines in the drawing, except perhaps the very longest, to be measured at once.

COMPARATIVE SCALES.

When the scale of a drawing is adapted to one unit of length, it is sometimes necessary to construct another scale, in which the unit is different. Such scales are called COMPARATIVE or CORRESPONDING SCALES.

If the unit of the proposed scale be a multiple, or a measure of the unit of the given one, the change is easily effected. When such is not the case, the length of the new scale may be determined, as shown in the following examples.

Ex. 5. A scale of French leagues is attached to a map of France: the distance between two places, known to be 25 leagues apart, is represented on this map by 3·75 inches. Construct the corresponding scale of English miles.

(1 French league = 4262·84 English yards.)

Let the scale represent 100 miles, and put x for the number of inches in its length. The representative fraction is evidently the same as that of the given scale.

$$\text{Then, 25 French leagues} = \frac{4262 \cdot 84}{1760} \times 25 \text{ English miles.}$$

$$\therefore \underset{\text{Eng. miles.}}{\frac{4262 \cdot 84 \times 25}{1760}} : \underset{\text{Eng. m.}}{100} :: 3 \cdot 75 : x,$$

$$\text{whence } x = \frac{3 \cdot 75 \times 100 \times 1760}{4262 \cdot 84 \times 25} = 6 \cdot 19 \text{ nearly.}$$

Divide a line 6·19 inches long into 10 equal parts, to show tens of miles; subdivide the first primary division into 10 equal parts, to show miles.

Complete the scale as in the preceding examples (Pl. IV. Fig. 12).

Ex. 6. To construct a scale of the Austrian fuss, comparative to *Ex. 1.*

$$(1 \text{ fuss} = \cdot34568 \text{ English yards.})$$

Let the scale be 15 fuss long, then 15 fuss $= \cdot34568 \times 15 \times 3$ English feet, and 24 feet are represented by 12 inches.

ft.   ft.   in.

$\therefore 24 : \cdot34568 \times 3 \times 15 : 12 :$ length of scale in inches.

in.   in.

whence the length $= \dfrac{12 \times \cdot34568 \times 3 \times 15}{24} = 7 \cdot 7778 = 7 \cdot 78$ inches nearly.

The scale is constructed as shown in Fig. 8, Pl. IV.

$$\text{Representative fraction} = \frac{7 \cdot 7778}{\cdot34568 \times 15 \times 3 \times 12} = \frac{1}{24}.$$

Ex. 7. A scale of Milanese miglios corresponding to *Ex. 2.*

$$(1 \text{ miglio} = 1 \cdot 0277 \text{ mile.})$$

The length of this scale will be determined in a manner differing somewhat from that adopted in the preceding examples, but based upon the same principles.

It is evident that 1 mile English has the same ratio to 1 miglio that a line which represents any number of English miles has to the line representing the same number of miglios. The proportion may therefore stand thus.—

Eng. miles.   Eng. miles.   in.

1   :   1·0277 :: 5 5 : number of inches representing 11 miglios.

inches.   inches.

$\therefore$ length of scale $= 5 \cdot 5 \times 1 \cdot 0277 = 5 \cdot 65235.$

Had it been required to represent any other number of miglios, as, for example, 15, the proportion might have stood :—

miles.   miles.   in.   in.   in.

$11 : 1 \cdot 0277 \times 15 :: 5 \cdot 5 : 7 \cdot 70775 = 7 \cdot 71$ nearly.

miles.   miles.   in.   in.

or thus, $2 : 1 \cdot 0277 \times 15 :: 1 : 7 \cdot 70775$.

The scale may be seen completed in Fig. 10, Pl. IV.

Ex. 8. A scale of French kilomètres comparative to *Ex.* 2.

(1 kilomètre $= \cdot 62138$ Eng. mile $= 1093 \cdot 63$ yards.)

miles.   miles.   in.

$2 : \cdot 62138 \times 20 :: 1$; number of inches representing 20 kilomètres $= 6 \cdot 2138$ inches.

DIAGONAL SCALES.

The scales, of which the construction and application have been explained, though very useful, are not well adapted for measuring minute distances. There is, however, another kind of scale, termed, from its construction, the DIAGONAL SCALE, by means of which this object can be accomplished with great accuracy.

The principle upon which the construction of these scales depends has been shown in Prob. VI. sol. 2 ; its application will be elucidated by an example.

Ex. To construct a diagonal scale to show hundredths of an inch full size.

Construction. Draw 11 equidistant parallel lines, $\frac{4}{80}$ of an inch apart (Pl. IV. Fig. 13), and rather more than 7 inches long; call these lines horizontals for convenience of reference. Draw a twelfth line at a little greater distance below the eleventh. Through eight points, in this last line, one inch apart, draw perpendiculars to meet the top line and cut all the others,—call these verticals. Subdivide the left hand primary division on the eleventh horizontal into ten equal parts. From the first point of subdivision on the left draw a straight line to the point in which the left hand vertical cuts the top horizontal; through each of the other points of subdivision draw lines parallel to this line, meeting the first horizontal, and cutting all the others,—call these lines diagonals. The scale being now constructed may be completed as shown in the figure.

Use.—*Ex.* 1. To take off 2·3 inches.

Placing the point of one leg of the dividers on the point in which the vertical 2 meets the uppermost horizontal, extend the other leg to the point in which the diagonal 3 meets the same horizontal. The distance between the points of the dividers will be 2·3 inches, as required.

Ex. 2. To take off 3·47 inches.

Placing one leg of the dividers at the intersection of the vertical 3 with the horizontal 7, extend the other to the point in which the diagonal 4 meets the same horizontal.

This distance will be 3 in. + ·07 in. + ·4 in. = 3·47 in. For on the horizontal 7 the distance from the vertical 3 to the vertical marked 0 is 3 inches; from this vertical to the diagonal marked 0 is $\frac{7}{100}$ inch; from diagonal 0 to diagonal 4 is $\frac{4}{10}$ inch.

The same method may be applied to any other horizontal.

EXAMPLES FOR PRACTICE.

1. Construct a scale of $\frac{1}{1760}$.

2. Construct a scale of 8·5 feet to an inch, to measure single feet.

3. A scale of 3·5 miles to 1·25 inch.

4. A scale of 5 fathoms to 1·5 inch.

5. A scale of mètres $\frac{1}{340}$. 1 mètre = 1·0936 Eng. yards.

6. Finding that the distance between two points on a Swedish map is 7 inches, and the real distance on the ground 5000 alners, construct for it a scale of feet; the alner being ·6498 of an English yard.

7. Draw a scale of 22 yards to an inch, 100 yards long, on which single yards can be measured.
Also a scale of toises comparative to the above. The toise· is equal to 76·731 English inches.

8. A scale of 5 miles to ·75 inch; and a corresponding. scale of Russian versts. 1 verst = 1166·68 yards.

9. Draw a scale of 13·36 yards to $\frac{4}{5}$ of an inch, 100 yards long.

10. Draw a diagonal scale to show 1000ths of a foot, full size.

11. Construct scales of Bavarian rods and Bavarian ells corresponding to 11·5 feet to an inch; the rod being equivalent to 3·1917 English yards, and divided into 10 feet, and the ell being ·74845 English yards.

12. A Prussian fathom contains 6 Rhenish feet, each 1·0297 English feet. Construct a scale of fathoms $\frac{3}{700}$, showing feet diagonally.

13. A scale of 7 feet to $\frac{7}{8}$ of an inch, showing inches by the diagonal method.

14. A scale of yards $\frac{1}{200}$, 40 yards long, and a corresponding scale of Russian archines. Archine = ·7777 of a yard.

15. An Englishman wishing to examine a Spanish plan, finds only a scale of Spanish palms, 20 to an inch; supply him with a corresponding scale of English feet, taking the palm as ·684 English foot. Show 50 feet.

16. Make a diagonal scale of 10 feet to 1·5 inch, showing inches diagonally, and explain the principle of the construction.

17. Draw scales of $\frac{3}{500}$ to represent English feet, French metres, and Greek cubits. 1 mètre = 3·27 feet; 1 cubit = ·45 mètre.

18. Draw a scale of 6 inches to a mile, to measure furlongs, and diagonally, spaces of 50 feet.

19. The distance between two towns on a Swedish map is 9·125 inches English, they are 120 Swedish miles apart. Con-

struct for this map a scale of English miles. 1 mile Swedish =
6·6412 English miles.

20. Construct comparative scales of English furlongs, and
Roman and Greek stadia.

> 1 furlong = 220 yards.
> 1 Greek stadium = 196·85 yards.
> 1 Roman stadium = 202·29 yards.

N.B. In every example where the representative fraction is not given,
calculate it.